POPULAR INDIAN MYTHOLOGICAL STORIES FOR KIDS

THIS BOOK BELONGS TO

LIST OF STORIES

- **RAMAYAN**

- **THE STORY OF GODDESS DURGA**

- **HIRANYAKASHYAP**

- **GANESHA GETS HIS ELEPHANT HEAD**

- **THE STORY OF ONAM**

- **SITA - BIRTH OF SITA**

RAMAYAN

RAMAYAN

Thousands of years ago in the city of Ayodhya, there is a wise and good king named Dasharatha, who rule along with his three queens and four Prince's. The eldest Ram has beautiful wife Sita. They lived happily along with the other Prince brothers and their wives.

But one of King Dashrath wives was jealous of Ram and demanded that he be exiled to the forest for 14 years, so that her son Bharat be made King.

Having once promised his wife to fulfill any wish of her, the helpless King exiled Ram to the forest and so Ram set off on foot accompanied by his loving wife Sita and loyal younger brother Lakshman.

A few years into the exile a demoness named Surpanakha saw Ram and fell for his looks. she asked him to marry her. Rama refused and asked her to go to Lakshman instead.

But Lakshman also refused and raged
Surpanakha showed her true form and Lakshman
cut off her nose and ears. The demoness went
wailing to her brother, who is none other than
Ravan, the demon king of Lanka.

Ravan was furious and swore revenge with the help of an undead demon who took the form of a golden deer. He distracted Ram and Laxman and kidnapped Sita from that Hut.

When Rama and Lakshman returned Sita was missing. They realized that something bad had happened while they were gone and immediately rushed to find her.

On their way they came across an army of monkeys and bears that agreed to help them. Among them there was a monkey named Hanuman, who once vowed to be a tram service. Now Hanuman was no ordinary monkey, he could fly over mountains and has superhuman strength, he had the power to leap across oceans in a single stride.

It was Hanuman who finally found Sita in prison in one of flowers beautiful garden. Hanuman reassured Sita the Ram would be here soon to rescue her. he came back to Ram. The army of monkeys, bears and men marched to Lanka.

Soon, a great battle started between the two mighty armies and Ram soldiers managed to kill all the demons except one Ravan. The battle was now between Ram and Ravan. He gave Ravan one last chance to apologize and return Sita. Ravan instead rain down weapons on him.

Ram fought back relentlessly, but despite all his efforts nothing seemed to kill Ravan. Finally, Ravan's brother Vibhishan told Ram that Ravan's weakest point was in his navel. Using an arrow given to him by the gods, Ram shot Ravan in the navel.

Instantly Ravan dies. Ram and Sita were finally reunited.

Soon after upon completion of their 14 years in exile, Ram, Sita and Lakshmana returned home to find the entire city waiting for them. The streets were decorated with flowers and lamps and there was happiness everywhere and this is why every year on the Diwali we see the streets, home and offices light up with lamps, like the city of Ayodhya in celebration of Rama and Sita's homecoming.

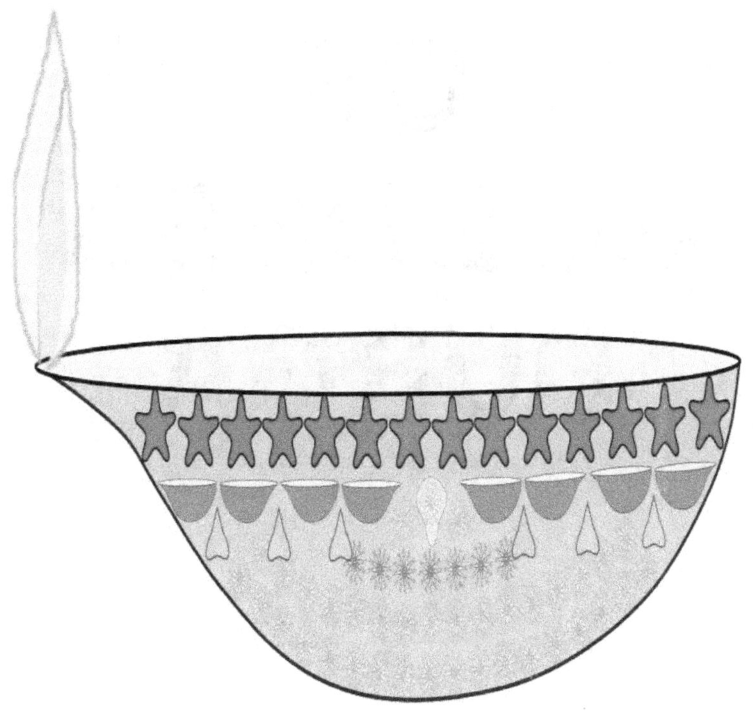

THE STORY
OF
GODDESS
DURGA

THE STORY OF GODDESS DURGA

Once upon a time there was a demon called Mahishasur. He was part demon and part buffalo. Mahishasur meditated for thousands of years, so he could please God Brahma and in return be blessed with immortality and power.

After much penance Lord Brahma came to him
and said
"I'm very pleased with your devotion. Ask me
any boon that you desire."

Without batting an eyelid Mahishasur said
"lord I don't want any man or God to be able to
kill me."

Brahma raised his hand in blessing and said
"Tatastu - so be it my child"

Mahishasura considered himself immortal, as no man or God could lay hands on him. Mahishasura started Killing innocent people, Rishi's mercilessly. He chased away the gods out of heaven. The gods went running to Brahma, Vishnu and Shiva and narrated that misfortune.

The Lord Brahma, Vishnu and Shiva hopping man they conferred for a moment and then they held each other and started to radiate a blinding light, a light never seen before. Out of this beautiful light was born the ten-armed goddess Durga, the embodiment of Adi Shakti.

One by one the gods approached her and gifted her dazzling array of weapons. the mighty Sudarshan chakra was given to her by Vishnu. She got a commander or pitcher from Lord Brahma. she got a quiver full of arrows from Lord Varuna the god of the sea. Lord Yama the god of death give her a powerful scepter. Lord Indra a thunderbolt to rattle the earth. Lord Vishwakarma a menacing axe. Time give her a sharp sword. Airavata Indra's white elephant give goddess Durga a bell, its noise helped to confuse the demons.

Lord Shiva give her a dangerous Trident. The mighty Himalayas give Goddess Durga anion to ride upon. She looked ready to show Mahishasur who the boss was and went into battle with him.

Goddess Durga fought with Mahishasura continuously for 10 Days. On 10th day Durga killed Mahishasura. To celebrate the victory, we perform Durga puja every. Durga Puja is a 10-day carnival in Bengal. This day is also called the Dussehra and we celebrate Lord Ram's victory over Ravana.

HIRANYAK ASHYAP

HIRANYAKASHYAP

This is the story of Holi. Holi gets its name from demon king Hiranyakashyap. Hiranyakashyap had got a boon from Lord Brahma that he would not be killed by man or animal at day or night, inside or outside, above or on the ground.

So Hiranyakashyap said that only he should be worshipped and not God. His own son Prahlad continued to worship Lord Vishnu. This made his father angry. He asked Prahlad to jump from a mountain, but he remained unhurt because he was Chanting Narayana Narayana when he was falling from the mountain.

Hiranyakashyap forced Prahlad to hard jump in a well, But then also Prahlad alive because of Chanting Lord Vishnu's name Narayana, Narayana.

Hiranyakashyap was unhappy, he ordered the wild elephants to crush Prahlad, but he was not hurt because of Chanting Lord Vishnu's name Narayana, Narayana...

Next Prahlad was put in a room with poisonous angry snakes, the poisonous snakes Couldn't do anything to Prahlad because he was chanting Lord Vishnu's name.

Finally, Hiranyakashyap had set Prahlad on a Fire, But Prahlad was safe from fire.

Then Hiranyakashyap become angry and he started breaking Pillars of his palace with his Golden weapon Gadha.

Lord Vishnu appeared as half-man and half-lion and killed Hiranyakashyap. bonfire is lit every year as the sign of victory of good over evil. Holi is celebrated on the day after the bonfire.

GANESHA GETS HIS ELEPHANT HEAD

GANESHA GETS HIS ELEPHANT HEAD

Hi my name is Ganesha and you probably see me everywhere. Do you know how I came to be? Well. Let me tell you.

Once upon a time high up in the Himalayas, my mother Parvati lived with her husband Shiva. One day my mother sat down to make a sculpture of a boy. She carefully molds the clay and ended up making a cute little boy. Chubby cheeks and everything.

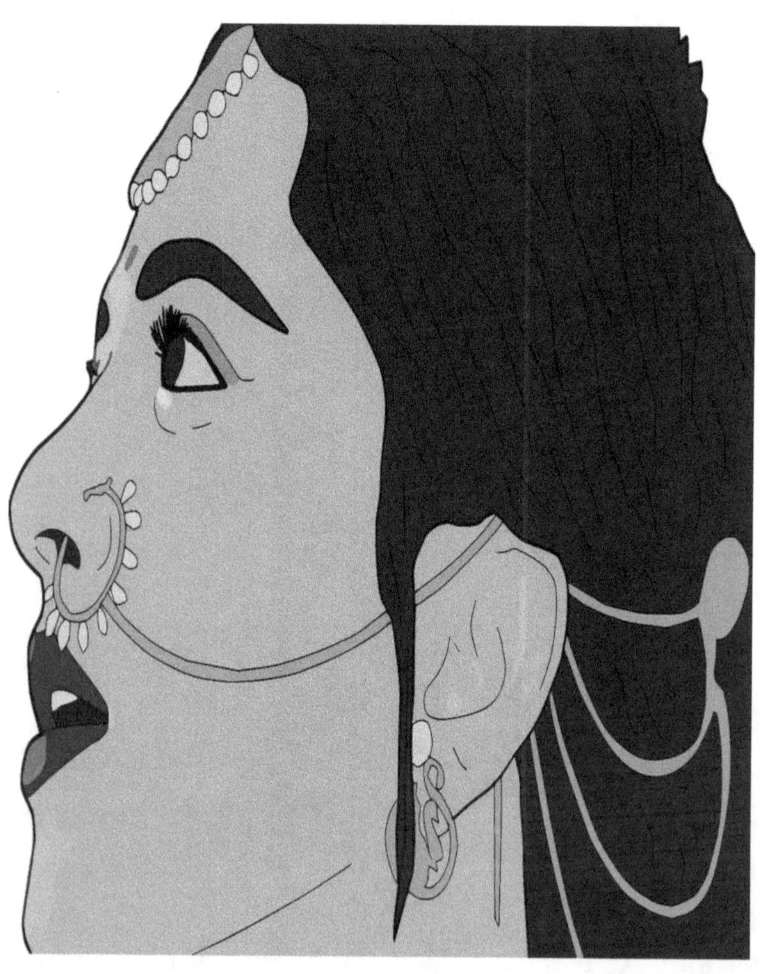

She was very pleased with her creation. So, she decided to give it life and this clay sculpture came to life. We were both ecstatic since my mother had gotten dirty from making me. She decided to take a bath, as my father the great Shiva was away. She told me to guard the door and not let any strangers in.

Now I've never seen Shiva as I was just born. I sat outside playing with the stick and minding my own business. When a large man, a blue and cool came up to the hut, not knowing who he was I stopped him and he said
"How dare you? I am Shiva."

In anger Shiva cut off my head. Haring the noise my mother came running out of the hut and said "what have you done to her son. I made him out of the earth with such love and you have gone and chopped his head off."

He promised my mother that he would find a suitable head for their little boy. So, he went into the forest. Shiva was back in no time. The head of an elephant which he fixed on to me. He then patted me and told me how proud he was of me. Honestly obeying my mother's orders and Shiva gave me blessings of prosperity and intelligence.

Since then I've been known by many many names as Vignadatha, Siddhivinayak and Ganapati and I remove all obstacle.

THE STORY
OF ONAM

THE STORY OF ONAM

Onam is a harvest festival in Kerala. Here's a story behind it. once upon a time the demon king Mahabali be ruled over Kerala. He was wise and fair king.

Mahabali worshipped Vishnu. His power extended to patala, the nether world and the heaven. The gods became jealous of Mahabali and all gods went to Lord Vishnu. Lord Vishnu took the avatar of Vamana, a Brahman. He approached Mahabali for the armors. He only wanted the land that he could cover in three steps. Mahabali agreed.

the Vaman began to grow in size and put his one step in the sky, with a second step Lord Vishnu covered the netherworld. Mahabali realized a lot of mysteries about Lord Vishnu, Lord Vishnu's third step would destroy the earth. So, he offered his head for Lord Vishnu.

His last step, when Lord Vishnu placed his foot on Mahabali's head and pushed him to the netherworld.

Before taking the third step though Lord Vishnu granted Mahabali a boon. Mahabali asked for boon that he wish to visit Kerala once a year. Lord Vishnu granted boon to Mahabali. This day is celebrated as Onam.

SITA - BIRTH OF SITA

SITA - BIRTH OF SITA

Long ago there was a king named Janaka. He was the king of the Videha dynasty and ruled over the kingdom of Mithila. He looked upon his people with great love and affection.

King Janaka's only cause of depression was the
fact that he had no children and he constantly
prayed to God for a child. One day while he was
blowing a piece of land to prepare it for
conducting a yagna, which means a spiritual
sacrifice. He found a golden gasket in which he
found a beautiful baby girl.

Land blowed by the yoke is called Sita and so he named the baby girl Sita. But the arrival of the baby, the King's good luck sword. His queen also gave birth to a daughter who was named Urmila. The royal couple brought up the children with great affection.

They gave them a good education. The two beautiful girls by their noble qualities good behaviour and intelligence grew up to become ideal princesses. One day sage Parashurama came to visit King Janaka. He carried a bow with him. He left it at the doorstep of the Royal Hall and went inside. Sita saw the bow, ran through it and began playing with it.

PARASHURAMA- King Janaka, look at your daughter. Ordinary people cannot lift this blow, only those with great physical strength can lift and handle the Vaishnava bow. I don't know how she is capable of lifting it.

JANAKA- This indeed is amazing guru ji. It is proof of the fact that Sita has been sent to us by the gods.

PARASHURAMA- Janaka only a truly noble, great and strong person can marry this girl. when she grows up, arrange a Swayamvara for her and let the most suitable person marry her.

JANAKA- Guru we found Sita and the golden casket. We also found a very heavy bow on the ground. It was so heavy that we had to use horses to pull it back to the hall.

PARASHURAMA- Marriage Sita to the person who breaks that bow.

JANAKA- Thank you for your advice guru. I will do as you say.

King Rama lift that heavy bow easily and married to the Princess Sita.

Thank You!